MW01248861

Heaven Touched Me

Heaven Touched Me

Rebecca A. Wilhite

BOOKS™

Whispering Voice Books

This is a work of fiction. Any resemblance to persons that you may know, living or dead, is purely your good luck.

Published by Whispering Voice Books
P.O. Box 981076 Park City, UT 84098

First printing 2002

Library of Congress Control Number 2002105842

ISBN 0-9720760-0-X

Printed in the USA

Typography by Heather Steed

If you see a piece of yourself in this book,
then I wrote it for you.

PREFACE

Heaven has touched me countless times. As an occasionally lonesome child, I never felt really alone. I had a Heavenly family near enough to be felt, but far enough away to remain unseen. At sixteen I lost my mother, and I was spared the ripping anguish that my life would end also. A spirit of peace entered my heart, and I felt that God would put His arm around me and fill my life with opportunities for feeling His love. I have been given incredible gifts of joy which are my husband and children, and when I feel so lucky that I may burst I feel the presence of unseen loved ones rejoicing with me.

God loves His children, and He wants us to help each other. I have been given a heart full of confidence in the mercy and kindness of a Father in Heaven who has a plan for our eternal happiness. I wanted to share that assurance. So I asked God how I could help Him heal the hearts of His struggling children, how I could share my trust in His love. Then He gave me Hannah. She bloomed before my eyes as a tremendous example of joy and hope and fun and faith. She made me chuckle and she made me cry, and she was just good enough to be true.

The book became a sketch of the person I want to be. Most people I know want to be kinder, more loving, more sharing; in Hannah I watched those characteristics come alive. Someone acted on the good intentions so many of us ponder. Hannah assumed her love would be accepted in the spirit that it was offered, and her goodness seemed more and more attainable with each act that opened itself to my view. As Hannah fought cancer her prevailing weapon was her ability to spot a need and fill it. Maybe the Lord gave me Hannah so I would consider the possibility of what I can become. Now I offer her to you.

Becca

It felt so cold.

Someone must have to try to make a room so comfortless, so unlike anyplace a person would choose to be. The antiseptic smells made Jim feel weak and dizzy, like maybe he should get a bed too. As he raised his exhausted head from his hands he saw Hannah's weak and helpless body motionless except for the occasional spasm of pain that even these enormous doses of morphine couldn't prevent. The room was colorless. Even the white blankets reflected the bluish non-color of intensive care rooms. As his eyes traveled from her bald head to her sunken cheeks to her thin, shrunken body under the blanket, he glimpsed the only real color in the room. Hannah's enormous red straw bag with the daisies on it. It was almost comical to see it here, so obviously out of place. But she never went anywhere unless she had that bag. ("Don't let me leave home without it," she had told him. He remembered.) Seeing her in this sterile, unfriendly place she looked like a different woman. At home she reflected the warmth and happy chaos she created so that even when she was sick, she was beautiful. He wished she would open her eyes one more time so he could see that sparkle he loved. If only she would laugh or even smile at him once more. But even if her eyes were to open, she could no longer see. The cancer in her brain had stolen her eyesight.

"Hannah. Please. Just open your eyes and look at me. Sing to me. Ask me what's for dinner. Call Kristen. Tell me a joke. Tell me a story. Tell me how in the world I am going to live without you."

She had tried to help him prepare for her death. She had known it was coming, but nothing she had said could make him ready to see her this way and feel this sickening helplessness. Reaching under the covers he found her hand and clenched it in both of his.

"Hannah. Remember when you got your diagnosis? You came to my office and said, 'Well, it's an inoperable brain tumor. But don't worry — it's all in my head.' You aren't that funny, you know. But you could always make me laugh. Make me laugh now. Make me roll my eyes. Make me feel alive again."

The gentle hand on his shoulder startled him awake.

"Hi, Daddy."

"Kristen, I'm glad you could come. What time is it?" He rubbed his eyes and stretched his kinked neck.

"It's 5:30. I just got off work. Curt is going to meet me here when he's finished. How long have you been sleeping?" She looked worried, so he lied.

"I just nodded off for a second. Why don't you sit here with Mom and I'll go grab us a drink." He gave her the closest thing to a comfortable seat that the room offered and helped her sit down. Getting into a chair was lately a challenge. He patted her round stomach and smiled at her. Suddenly overcome with awe for his little girl and the life she was carrying inside her, he leaned over and kissed Kristen's forehead.

"Want some juice? I'll be right back."

As he walked down the long hall towards the cafeteria, Jim tried to rouse himself to feel positive. He knew Kristen was dealing with a pain as strong as his along with anger that he simply did not understand. He had felt strengthened by his faith during the last months. In his heart he knew that he and Hannah would meet again after her death. But then death had been a theory, a distant, unreal place on the horizon. Now that it was becoming such an encompassing reality he wondered if his faith was strong enough to see him through. He found an unoccupied room and let himself inside. Closing the door softly, he knelt beside the empty bed.

"Dear Father, please help me. I know You love Hannah as much as I do. But I need her. She has been the focus of my life for twenty-six years. I don't know how to act without her. I believe that You must need her there with You, or You wouldn't take her from me. Without her I will be half a man. How can I keep her memory in my heart when I can no longer hold her in my arms? Father, please help me. Please strengthen my faith. Please help me remember that Hannah and I will be together again. Please help me to see that her work is finished. I know she is ready to go. Please give me the strength to say goodbye for this last time."

An aching sob wrenched out of Jim's tight throat and he pressed his face into the blanket. His shoulders shook and his eyes burned. Then suddenly years of memories flooded his mind. He saw birthday parties and campouts, soccer games and road trips, quiet evenings in the porch swing and Hannah's beautiful smile. And he heard laughter. His ears practically rang with the memory of Hannah's laugh. He took a deep breath and raised his head.

"Father, please let me always hear her laughter. You know how that laugh could always heal my heart. Please bring that precious sound to my mind, and I will know that she is laughing in her new Home. Dear Father, please let me keep my Hannah in my heart after she is back in Your arms."

As he stood to leave, Jim felt he was standing a little taller. And somehow he didn't feel quite as cold anymore.

❖

Jim pushed the door open with his elbow as he held two cups of orange juice in his hands. He stopped just inside the door when he heard Kristen's voice.

"Why did you promise? Why did you even say that you'd be here when you had no control? You promised you'd be with me when this baby comes, and now you won't and it's not fair. People like you aren't supposed to die. You are the one that makes life good for the rest of us. What am I supposed to do now? I don't know how to be a mom. I am terrified that I'll mess up with this kid and there will be no one to blame but me. Mom, I need you. The baby needs a grandma."

As Jim quietly circled around the back of Kristen's chair, he saw that she was holding Hannah's hand against her round belly. He set down the juice and came up beside her. He put his hand next to Hannah's and met Kristen's watery eyes. He felt the baby move and smiled. Kristen tried to smile back, but the tears came instead.

"Dad, I'm sorry. I don't mean to be angry and awful.

I know I'm being selfish and I can't help it. I feel like I'm about to be pushed into the blackest darkness. It feels like I'm four years old again, and I want my Mommy." As the tears streamed down her face, Jim stroked her hair. He wanted to pass on the comfort he now felt in his heart, but he knew no words for it. He laid his head against Kristen's and silently prayed for his daughter.

On 2 October 2001 we said goodbye to **HANNAH LOUISE STANTON.** The memory of her smile and laughter will live forever in our hearts. The cancer that took her life didn't change the kindness that characterized each of her days, except perhaps by giving her an urgency to show her love to each of us.

She is survived by her husband Jim, her daughter Kristen (Curt) Baines, her father Joseph Knight, her brother Matthew Knight and countless loved ones.

Services will be at Braeburn Funeral Home on Saturday the 6th at ten o'clock. In lieu of flowers, please bring a letter for the family's memory book.

Dear Miss Hannah,

I will miss you. I will miss the hot chocolate and snickerdoodles on my way home from school. You always said nice words to me. I think it's neat that you wanted to be my friend.

Our street will feel different without you, but I bet I can learn to cook snickerdoodles just as good as you did.

Mommy said you're an angel now, and I didn't tell her she was wrong, but I'm pretty sure you always were.

Love,

Lindsey

Dear Jim and Kristen,

Hannah was the dearest friend and neighbor anyone could have. It seems funny that it's entirely possible to live on the same block and be strangers. That couldn't happen with Hannah around. She hosted block parties and arranged summer barbecues. She saw to it that every baby was celebrated, every new family was welcomed, no kind word was left unsaid and no special event went unnoticed. She made our neighborhood a family and she became, if not the mother, at least our favored aunt.

I have certainly received more than my share of loving acts. Even more than the kindness that she showed my family, I now appreciate the times she took me along to help someone else. She showed me how to act on my good intentions.

Any number of people could have done what Hannah did; most seem to prefer doing these things in anonymity. That would have been my way, too; but Hannah taught me the sweetness of allowing your neighbor the opportunity to say "thank you." And never was there a more gracious "you're welcome" than the very simple squeeze of the hand and smile which accompanied her visits of goodwill. And somehow when she said "It's my pleasure" we all believed that it truly was.

Although she didn't know about her cancer until this year, something tells me that she was preparing me all this time, all these years, to be able to step in and offer my own form of "love you can see" through our neighborhood and beyond.

There are things Hannah did that I will never be great at, but I'm developing my own talents that can be shared. I imagine quite a few people are wondering what might be done to fill the void Hannah's death has left. If even a few of us find some way to live life more fully and more kindly, be less hectic and less selfish, then Hannah's influence can grow exponentially.

The world is a crazy place, certainly. But just as sure, there are plenty of people who would be happy to show some goodness if they had an example to follow. I'll follow Hannah, and maybe my Lindsey will follow me. Hannah would laugh aloud if anyone suggested to her that she changed the world, but she certainly changed my world — and I'll bet many people feel that way.

Denise

Dear Stantons,

Of all the wonderful memories and experiences our family has had with Hannah, none matches the feeling of love we had for her at the onset of Jacob's deafness. When every friend, neighbor and family member was phoning or visiting to tell us they didn't know what to say, Hannah stopped over one afternoon with a list of names. She had spent what was probably no more than a few minutes doing a bit of research, and presented us with several options where a family could learn sign language together. It was exactly what we needed.

At a time when shock and sadness denied me the ability to act as a father should, Hannah gave me a gentle push in the one useful direction. Of all the kind things she'd done for us through the years, this probably took the least effort; but it was certainly the most sensitive and helpful offering made to us at a time of family crisis.

And then she'd check up on us. She let Jacob teach her a few signs, and always waved the "I love you" sign when she saw him. Because she was the first to introduce the idea of signing to our family, she will always be a part of our communication and therefore our relationships. How lucky we all have been to have had a part in Hannah's life.

Love,

The Watsons

Jim,

When I started my landscaping business, I used my back yard as an outdoor showroom. I'd use different groupings and move things around now and then to try new products and designs. One afternoon when I came home from work, Jeanne told me we were having a party in the back yard. When? I asked. She didn't know. Who's coming? She didn't know that either. So who did you invite — or don't you remember that either? She told me she didn't invite anybody. Hannah Stanton was planning a neighborhood barbecue, and she volunteered our yard because it was the prettiest around. (She knew how to get us to say yes!) With all the traffic through the yard, I got several projects because of that party. But more important, we met people that we now call friends.

Bryant Elkins

Miss Hannah,

Last year in fifth grade I was having trouble with fractions. My mom sent me over to talk with you. You asked me what was giving me trouble, and sat down at the table with me. Then you got out two apples and cut the first one in ten pieces. You arranged the slices in piles, and showed me "halves" and "fifths" and "tenths." You cut the other one in twelve pieces, and showed me "fourths" and "thirds." Your explanation made lots of sense to me, and even though I'm not the smartest one in my math class, I do really well at fractions now.

Ty Bradford

Mr. Stanton,

Late in July of '98 two weeks before our second child was born we got a phone call. It was Hannah asking if we had any plans for the weekend. When we told her no, she said, "Now you do. Go see a movie and let me come play with your Jamie." Idiots that we were, we actually tried to say no; but she wouldn't hear of it, convincing us that it would be quite some time before we'd be able to go out on a date again after the baby arrived. So we went and of course had a wonderful time, and since then we've tried to give our friends who are second time parents one last date before baby number two makes an appearance. It's such a simple thing to do, but it made a great memory for us. And we're happy to make it a family tradition.

The Kings

To Hannah's Family:

"Well, I made it anyway, and it's just not going to be as good tomorrow." That's what Hannah told me one winter afternoon as she stood on my doorstep with homemade soup and bread. I had been home with a nasty cold, feeling lousy, looking worse — and Hannah just seemed to know about it. "It just felt like a day to spend in the kitchen." Not to me, that's for sure. "So now dinner's ready, and you can go take a nap until Bradley gets home." She handed over the goods and headed for home. Now, I am no chef but whenever I make cookies I like to take a plate full to a neighbor and say, "It's just not going to be as good tomorrow."

Hannah was always running around being an inspiration to people — showing us that it's no big thing to show a little kindness.

Gretchen Sanders

Dear Kristen,

I'm so sorry to hear about your mom. What a thing, to lose a mother — especially now that you're about to become a mom too.

I've been thinking about all the old times — the glory days of silly female adolescence — and how "Ma Hannah" was so great for us. Remember the Summer of the Lemonade Stand? I think we spent every day for two weeks constructing a "sales counter" with a dazzling marquee on that green chalkboard and a cardboard cash register. The day we finished our preparations began the Great Monsoons of '88. I don't believe, now that I look back on it, that it actually rained every day for a month, but it sure felt like it, didn't it? Never the ten-year-olds to be daunted, we'd mix our lemonade and sell it to Ma Hannah. The irony of her buying the lemonade twice was lost on us kids; she was our main supplier as well as our best and most loyal customer (and the greatest tipper).

Remember the Dramatic Club? She got half the neighborhood involved in that one. Angie's mom was installed as playwright and my mom was volunteered as costume mistress (because she confessed to making some of our clothes — I wonder if she regretted that admission). Ma Hannah was director and cookie provider. She got your dad to make that stage in the back yard — with working curtains. And didn't they rent a spotlight from the high school? We all felt like stars, didn't we?

Remember the winter that we tried to teach her to ice skate? We had her drive us down to the rink; we told her it wouldn't be too cold inside, but she insisted on wearing that awful hat with the pom-pom on top which came right out of the seventies (the mark of death for us) and we were mortified. (Meanwhile, we're each wearing earrings the size of small planets, which were oh-so-cool and I'm sure she was rolling her eyes at our own fashion statement). We dragged her out on the ice, and she actually took to it pretty well, but she was determined to embarrass us to the fullest extent and started doing all these moves that she claimed were Olympic-caliber and bowing to the imaginary judges. It became unbearable when people began clapping and cheering and pretty soon the whole rink full of people got into her game. I think the only two people in the place who weren't laughing were hiding under a bench with their huge earrings and very red faces. When she sat down for a rest, you suggested that maybe she was cold and needed some hot chocolate. She insisted on "buying drinks for the silver and bronze medallists." We all took a victory lap around the rink, blushing like crazy while she grinned, held up our arms, and hummed the national anthem. As much as we thought we'd die of humiliation, even then we had to admit it was funny. She may not have been cool in the way moms who watched MTV were cool, but she always seemed to love hanging out with us. Of course at the time, we mostly wished her away, but I adore those memories. I treasure my childhood with you, and Ma Hannah was such a part of it. I'm so sorry you lost her; I am so glad I had a chance to love her.

Love,

Beth

Dear Hannah,

In the two and a half years that Kristen and I have been married I never have been comfortable calling you Mom. Some people can do that with the in-laws, I'm just not one of those people. But I hope you have never doubted my admiration and respect for you. You and Jim have consistently shown how great marriage can be when based on love, friendship, respect, honesty and fun. Together you created Kristen and helped her become the most amazing person I know. You instilled in her values and morals and principles that we want to pass on to our children. It's about our children that I need to write. Kristen is of course, heart-broken to lose you. But beyond that I think she is afraid to be a mom without your help.

I know she'll be amazing. She already loves this baby more than I can believe. It's hard for me to comprehend the connection Kristen already feels. But now the fear of the impending arrival sets in.

In a few weeks this child is going to appear to two very inexperienced and nervous parents. And I would feel a lot better if I thought you'd be involved somehow. Send a little courage our way, a little confidence, and a lot more faith. I just want you to know that I'll do my best by Kristen and this baby. I'll be the husband Kristen deserves and the dad this baby needs.

Love,

Curt

Dear Kristen,

When I first met your mom I was dating Uncle Jared and we came to your parent's place for Easter dinner. You were maybe eight months old, crawling all over that dank basement apartment. She called it "The Cavern" and professed to love it. Later I understood how you can love a place because of what happens in it without regard for what it looks like (or smells like!). Our newlywed apartment was, in hindsight, hideous — but the memories of our first three years there are golden.

So it was Easter, and my first impression of your mom was something like "Wow, I had no idea a person could do that with a hard-cooked egg." Easter dinner consisted of one very small ham, deviled eggs, egg salad, potato salad (heavy on the eggs), chef's salad and little decorated-egg place settings. I bet there were a dozen eggs for each of us. During dinner, though, I noticed that your mom didn't serve herself any of the side dishes. She didn't even eat a single deviled egg. There was obviously enough to go around, so I kept passing plates to her. She passed them right along. Finally, I got up the courage to ask if she was going to have any egg salad and she said, "No way. I hate hard boiled eggs." I was baffled. "Why did you make all of this?" I asked her. "It's Kristen's first Easter. I wanted to do it right, so we had a huge egg hunt this morning. I sure hope we found them all, or the Cavern is going to have to be renamed Sulfur Shack!"

You weren't old enough to hunt eggs, certainly too young to care. But she worked hard to make it special for you. I knew then that if I were ever a mom I'd have a good role model in Hannah. I hope you can find some comfort now in the memories and the years that she spent putting you and your dad first. You are very lucky to never need wonder what your mother's top priorities and greatest loves were.

Love,

Aunt Sam

Jim,

It has always been a treat being your neighbor, but especially lately. When my brother was sick with cancer and weakening, he wanted no help. He shut us out of the end of his life. I think it was wonderful that Hannah let me come and visit her and do her dishes and change the linens. I'm an old lady, and you know an old lady needs someone to fuss over. I was thrilled that Hannah would let me fuss over her. I can't do much, but I can make one mean hospital corner. Once when I was visiting with Hannah and cleaning some dishes, I asked her if there were many things she hadn't been able to do yet in her life that she had really wanted to do (one of the privileges of old-ladyhood is being able to ask very bold personal questions) and she told me she had never sung on the stage. "Broadway?" I asked her. No, it didn't matter what stage, just a stage. So I cleared the coffee table, helped her stand up on it, sat on the couch and told her to go for it. She giggled and blushed and began to sing. Show tunes, lullabies, old jazz numbers. For an hour she sang until she said she couldn't stand up for the dizziness. I clapped and cheered; she bowed graciously. It was a delight to be able to grant one little wish for someone who always considered other peoples' dreams before her own.

What a joy to have had such a friend. She would have made a super old lady, you know. But she managed to pack years of care-taking and fussing-over into every visit and encounter. If I live to be a hundred and six, I bet I won't have affected so many people in so many ways.

Love,

Mabel

Stanton Family,

There are some customers that you wait for and get attached to. I've been running Dewey's nursery for years and every spring, summer and fall Hannah would come in and give us a laugh. Sometimes she'd hear of some bizarre flower and drill us on it: Can it grow here? Sun or shade? Will it work in an arrangement? Then she'd laugh at us for stumbling through the books and say, "Oh you know I'm a basics girl," and she'd buy pansies or daisies, petunias or daffodils. She loved to tell us how her trees were coming. I think she must have gotten on a ladder to measure them before she'd make a trip to see us.

When she came in September for bulbs, she brought a

friend with her to help find the "right red" for the garden. It had to be exactly the color of her big straw bag with the daisies on it. Her friend said, "Why do you care what shade of red they are? You're not even going to see them." Quietly she said, "Jim will." She picked out, and I imagine went home and planted, flowers she would never see. The world would be a lovelier place if more people planted seeds for others to enjoy.

Jarome Dewey

Dewey's Nursery

Mr. Stanton,

Your wife was certainly something. When she first came in and asked me to locate the source of her morning sickness, I was impressed by her positive attitude. And later when I presented the diagnosis, I asked if she would care for an estimate of her timeline. I will never forget her response. She looked me straight in the face and said, "I know exactly how long I have left — every day for the rest of my life." And she smiled.

As a doctor, I wish there were a way I could prescribe that kind of attitude for my other patients. The difference in outlook has a tremendous effect on physical feeling. If nothing else, someone who expends such energy during the day sleeps better at night. But there was something else. She knew she was going to die, but she decided to let Death chase her down, not find her waiting in her rocker. Maybe she was too good to be true, but she was a ray of light in a place of sadness. And I hope some of my other patients have carried something of her positive, happy outlook away into every day of the rest of their lives.

Dr. James Tait

To Hannah's Family:

When Hannah came into my life, God became real. All of life became more meaningful. She showed me the bigger picture; once I saw it, struggles became opportunities and coincidences became blessings. When she laughed, the angels sang. When she cried, stars fell. When she put her hand out, heaven touched me.

Grace

Dear Hannah,

After the first two accidental meetings in the doctor's waiting room, you suggested we make our appointments together. You always saved a seat for me with that crazy bag of tricks. My heart broke a little when you weren't there waiting.

Will you save me a seat in heaven?

Diego

Jim,

We had all the usual brother and sister times. I taught her how to throw a football, and she helped me get dates. When we were kids I used to very quietly torment her until she'd scream at me; then she'd get in trouble for shouting. I had that particular trick down to a science, but for some reason she fell for it every time. Now, of course, I can recognize it for what it was — she was forgiving me. Even though I was a big, mean brother she'd still play with me, and on my terms.

As I look back on the years she spent a lot of time forgiving. She forgave me when I went away for school and didn't come home for three years. She forgave Mom for dying too young. And I think she even forgave herself for her own physical limitations. She always thought she was superhuman and could do things that we ordinary mortals never could. At six she almost convinced me she could fly (until she jumped off the cab of Dad's old white Chevy truck and broke her leg). She was always sure it was possible to figure out anything, put together anything, or create anything. There wasn't a cookie in the bakery that she didn't try to copy, and she occasionally came pretty close.

A lot of people talk about overcoming personal limitations, but Hannah could really do it (except for the flying). Maybe it's true. Maybe we could all be what she was. Maybe our challenges can be overcome by our attitudes. Cancer was no easier for her than for anyone else, but life was different because of her outlook. She chose to look outside herself and not ignore, but simply accept, what was happening inside her. As my sister, she will always be in my heart. As an example of living a good life, she will never be forgotten.

Matthew

Mr. Stanton,

We have never met, but I feel like I know you very well. Your wife came through my checkout aisle at the market every Thursday morning for three and a half years. She knows the names, ages and medical records of all three of my sons. She recommended the very best children's books for Christmas gifts. Those books are priceless treasures at our house.

I have never seen anyone else get so excited when mangos were on sale. "Two for a dollar!" she'd say, and her face would light up. I asked her once why she always bought mangos. She smiled that shy smile of a schoolgirl with a crush, and told me that her husband loved mango-and-yogurt shakes. She said she'd perfected the art. I wouldn't have had a clue what to do with a mango, but she showed me how the feel of it, not the color, determines ripeness and suggested that now I knew the secret, I'd better give the shake a try. It's now the favorite treat for my boys, outranking cookies and ice cream.

I looked forward to Thursdays for the company, the smile and the stories. She was so positive about everything and so concerned and considerate to everyone. She noticed every time I had a cold. But it was not until your daughter had been shopping with her for a month that I started to realize that Hannah wasn't seeing things. She acted exactly the same, but she wasn't quite making eye contact anymore. I was embarrassed to say anything, but finally I asked her if she wasn't able to see so well. She smiled almost apologetically and told me that she had a "little friend" who had taken up residence in her brain and made it hard for her eyes to do their thing. "But I can still pick a perfect mango!"

She only came one more Thursday after that. There aren't too many people who carry on a real conversation in a grocery line, even though so many of us recognize each other. If we talk, it's always small talk and usually complaining. But Hannah was different, and I'll always remember that difference.

Susan Kramer

Mr. Stanton,

What a special woman your Hannah was. As she came for treatments, she would ask how we were feeling. All the nurses loved to help with Hannah. She'd always offer us gum or mints or a cookie out of that big red bag. She was so positive and cheerful. I'm sure she didn't always feel that way, but she'd act as happy as could be to come to treatment.

I've seen it happen before: the pain becomes secondary to the mission that must be fulfilled. And her mission was to bless the lives of every person in her path. Of course she suffered. But instead of dwelling on her pain, and focusing on the hand that she'd been dealt, she not only considered the ways she could help and serve her neighbors, but she acted on her ideas. How many people can say they've spent every day of their lives in kindness? At least one.

Naomi Dugan

Dear Uncle Jim,

I was just remembering when I was pregnant with Jack, and Ellie was two and into everything. I would just sit exhausted on the couch counting down the hours till Ellie's nap. I thought I'd never make it through those weeks. I'd just read Dr. Seuss until my lips were numb. Then one morning there was a knock on my door. It was Aunt Hannah, saying she thought I could use a break. She bounded up the stairs singing Ellie a song and drew me a hot bath. Then she pulled a book out of her big straw bag and said, "I don't want to see you back down here until you've had a nice bath and a rest." When I came downstairs two hours later, the house was spotless, lunch was on the table (served on Great Grandma's china — a girls' tea party!) and Ellie was having the time of her life. We ate lunch, Ellie went down for a nap and Aunt Hannah sat me down on the couch. She rubbed my shoulders, told me funny stories about when I was little, painted my toenails pink, and told me I was beautiful. She helped me prepare dinner — a double batch of lasagna so one could go into the freezer for another hectic day — and then she went home. It was evening by the time I realized she must have left her house at 6 a.m. and put in three hours on the road each way. What a gift that was. For weeks Ellie would watch out the front window when she heard cars in the street. I'm sure she was hoping for another magic day like that one.

Now that I consider it as an entire day out of Aunt Hannah's life, I feel terribly lucky to have spent it with her — that she would have spent it with me. Thank you for sharing her with us.

Love,

Heather

Jim,

Judy was recently in the hospital recovering from a surgery. Two weeks ago Mrs. Brady from the neighborhood dropped a fruit basket at our house. I began to thank her with surprise since she doesn't know our family very well. She denied the need for thanks. According to her, Hannah had phoned and asked her to come for a visit. She had agreed and asked if there were anything she could pick up for Hannah at the market. Glad to be asked, Hannah responded with a rather lengthy and specific shopping list. When Mrs. Brady got to your home, Hannah greeted her warmly and placed her at the kitchen table for a talk. Hannah set about putting fruits in a basket and chatting. When Hannah was ready to tie a bow on the completed fruit basket she asked Mrs. Brady to do the art direction. She then dictated a card and asked Mrs. Brady if she knew where our family lived. She said yes and Hannah commissioned her for delivery service. She brought the lovely fruit basket to our home. When Judy came home the next day she was delighted and surprised to see the gift. It seems amazing to us that Hannah would have spent even her last weeks thinking of us and how she could help. We are sorry for your loss, and we will certainly be here for you whenever you need a friend.

Howard

Hannah,

When you were still here with us, you knew where you were going. I wish I knew it too. Where are you now? Is it possible that you really are with God? If anyone ever knew Him, it's you.

Do you think He knows me?

Chris

My little girl,

How I wish it could have been me instead. You were so very full of life; but that was a choice you made, wasn't it? You decided to give your life to every person in your path, and in so doing, gave every day to God.

You were always a delight to me, but when you married Jim a new light showed in your eyes. Living for someone else's happiness created a new joy in you. Then when Kristen was born, your light increased. Certainly being a wife and a mother was not an easy task; but through the years you did it with such love and excitement I thought your joy must be full. But as I have watched you spend your last few months in service not only to your family but to everyone you had a chance to love, I realize that in a heart like yours, there is always room for more happiness, peace, love and delight. As your body became weaker the strength of your soul became ever more apparent. As your eyesight dimmed, your beautiful eyes began to radiate a love beyond the bounds of mortality. All who had the gift of knowing you and being loved by you felt the Divine in your presence.

And now that you're safe and whole in the presence of our Father, perhaps when those whose lives you touched stop to think of you, they will feel not only the love you shared with them, but also the True Source of that love. Perhaps the loss will not feel such a loss, but rather a trade — we gave up an angel for the knowledge of God.

Love,

Dad

Mr. Stanton,

All the staff at the library wanted to let you know how much we appreciated Hannah being our Story Time Lady. For eighteen months she's been a huge hit with the kids. Did you know we had to change story time locations twice to accommodate her standing-room only crowd? She gave the children of this community not only the gift of books and learning, but also a taste of the magic of a great imagination. Do you remember the time last summer that she presented some books about flowers and came dressed as a bee? Or at Christmas she wore an elf hat and gave all the children a pencil and a little notebook so they could write their own stories? My favorite, though, was when she would make up stories using the names of the kids in the circle. They would feel so important that she knew them, and their characters in her stories were always so noble and great. She was an inspiration to us all. She will certainly be greatly missed by the staff and all the children.

Sincerely,

Linda Martinez

Hannah,

I knew that it had been too long since I'd called or visited. I was busy with work and projects and everything that gets in the way. Then when I heard you were sick, I was embarrassed. I didn't want you to think that I was coming just for a "charity visit" or that I was curious to see how you looked without your hair. But I did want to see you. I wanted to talk with you. I wish that I had made the time. I know that I could have made the phone call. I shouldn't have waited to figure out what I'd say. I waited too long and I missed the chance to tell you how I felt about you. I'm sorry that I didn't come to say goodbye. I wanted to tell you that you have been a good friend all these years and that your sense of humor always brightened my day. Why didn't I make time for you? I wish I could know that you forgive me. Life passes too fast. I hope if I ever get the chance to say goodbye to a friend again that I will not let anything become more important. I didn't tell you while you could have heard me, but I need to tell you now. You were a dear friend, and I will always love you.

Kim

Jim,

I was just remembering when Lindsey was born and Denise was having a struggle with depression. Hannah came over one morning and asked Denise for some help. I think Denise was very surprised to be asked, but she said sure. Hannah explained that she was working on an experiment; she had several types of daisies growing in her flower garden and she wanted to know which type lasted longest after it was cut. She made this arrangement with Denise — Hannah would bring over a vase of cut daisies, and Denise should call her when they began to wilt. The day that happened, she'd bring a bowl full of a different variety. This continued through the whole summer. I'm sure having fresh flowers in the kitchen every day made a big difference in Denise's outlook. One day in the spring Hannah showed up with a nursery flat in her arms. She presented Denise with six types of daisies to plant in our yard saying, "Thanks for your help with the research. Turns out they're all good."

Those plants have brightened our garden, our kitchen, and the homes of friends for seven summers. I'm sure they will always remind us that it's not so hard to be a good neighbor. You just do what you can with a smile. And then you do it again.

Ray

Mom,

I'm sorry. I love you, and I feel like I spent your last days being angry with you. I kept thinking "she has no idea how abandoned I feel" and now that you're actually gone, I don't feel nearly so alone.

Your funeral was a hit. You'd have loved it. Sell-out crowd and everything. Mom, I miss you terribly and I am scared out of my mind to have my baby. But I think everything will be okay. Dad is being faithful and wonderful and so, of course, people are concerned about him. I won't mention any names, but there are those who are sure he's in denial. Why do you think it's impossible for people to understand his faith? But last week it was nearly impossible for me to understand your faith; now I guess I've found some peace. As I went to the funeral I was so wrapped up in feeling sad and lonely and deserted. But as I sat waiting for the service to begin, I prayed for reassurance. It was just like you always told me. "Ask and you'll receive." I felt comforted and calm. I think God really heard me.

I will still feel lonely for you, and I'm sure the sadness will still make me cry. But if I can focus on what a great blessing it has been to be your daughter, and if I can learn even half of the things you tried for all those years to teach me, I'll be all right.

The outpouring of love at your funeral made me realize that you were something special. Of course I think so because you're my mom, but now it seems like the whole world knew it better than I did. You just went ahead loving us all and doing nice things even after you got sick. And when people would ask you whether you should take it easy, you said, "Why? Because I'm dying? We're all dying, honey. Who knows? I may outlast you." You were right — although nobody liked to hear it — we are all dying. But you knew how to live. Thank you for being a good example to me and for raising me and for loving me. I feel like you understood when I was having a hard time accepting your death, and now I feel like I'm going to be okay. I love you, Mom. I'm glad you shared your life with me.

Kristen

My Hannah,

I know how you hate it when I get all sentimental, but face it, this letter is for my healing. Your pain is finished now. Your body is whole, your spirit is as strong as ever, and knowing you as I do, you're itching to keep up the good work.

I know I can't bring you back. Our home echoes without you. Nothing can fill that empty place in my heart except the hope that you're not so far away after all. That even if you're out of my sight, maybe I'm not out of yours. That our loving Father will let you keep an eye on me. All those people you loved, all those friends whose lives you touched are wearing your fingerprints on their hearts.

You have given pieces of yourself to everyone you've served. By staying near to them I can feel ever close to you. I will always see your smile in a daisy. I will always listen for your laugh, because there is no sound more beautiful in all the world. I will hear it in a crowded room and I will feel your happiness pour into me. And then when I see you again, we will laugh together and we will again be one.

While you were still with me, your death was merely an idea. I learned to accept that idea until it became insupportably real. As a reality it just hurt. I needed faith to accept the certainty of our separation. But now that death is a fact, I find that my faith — which was an idea — has become more real. The memory of you and the idea of you stay with me, and my faith that you are among the angels lifts my spirits daily. My faith grows stronger and it brings me hope. May God keep you in his watchful care until that wonderful day when my work, too, is finished and I can come home to you both.

Ever,

Jim

My dear ones,

I have loved being involved with you and being close to you. Nothing in the world could be as great as having so many people to love.

How I hope I have not made you sad. If I have hurt your feelings or been unkind, please forgive me. I have only meant to be a friend. If you feel sorry that I had to go, think how much sorrier I am that I left! But I will watch over you from my new lofty perch. I'll check up on you and make sure that you're all okay.

Many of you asked me why this cancer had to happen to me. I've struggled with this same question. I do have one very simple answer: I don't know. What I do know is that my trial has brought me closer to God. I had always been the praying kind — but not like I've prayed these last few months. Strange as it may sound I'm actually grateful for this cancer (not that I would wish it on anyone). For in my darkness and times of despair I have come to know and trust God. When my "little friend" took away my eyesight, God taught me to see with my heart. I think the words to one of my favorite hymns says it best:

Nearer, my God, to thee, nearer to thee
E'en though it be a cross that raiseth me.
Or if, on joyful wing cleaving the sky,
Sun, moon, and stars forgot, upward I fly,
Still all my song shall be nearer, my God, to thee,
Nearer, my God, to thee, nearer to thee.

It doesn't matter what brought me closer to Him, but it matters very much that I know Him better. I am not afraid to go Home.

Some people in my position may wonder if they were

a success in life. I doubt anyone would think my life was much to cheer about, but I've sure had a lot of great fun. Take care of each other, and maybe, once in a while, think of me. Now it's time for me to say goodbye — for now. How I look forward to the time we will see each other again.

Love and Kisses,

Hannah

Acknowledgements

Thanks to those who helped me do this fun project. To Scott, who has Midas eyeballs — he sees everything I do as though it were gold. Thanks to my girls: to Jana, who heard me call something a great book and asked, "Did you write it?" and to Kate, who said, "I'll buy it!" and to Ellie, who snuggled into one arm while I held a pen in the other. A thousand thanks to Amy, my cherished editor, who has waited this long to get paid. Thanks to Jason, for believing and making it happen. And Heather, who let me "pick her brain" (her words) about inoperable tumors, and who lives her life beautifully every day.

Thanks to all the Hannah Women I have known. Your lives are happy because you live for others. You find joy in the service of your families and neighbors, and we are blessed through you.

And to my Dad, whose unanticipated speechlessness was the best indicator of his love of the story.

COMING SOON —— THE MOVIE

We hope you've enjoyed meeting Hannah through the eyes of her friends. Now experience her as seen from a different view — her own. Whispering Voice Productions proudly presents *Upward I Fly,* the personal story of Hannah Stanton. We invite you to see what happens when life is near its end, but hope is not.

To preserve the integrity of the story, *Upward I Fly* is being made as an independent film and will be available on DVD and videocassette for home purchase. If you would like to be informed of its upcoming release, please visit

www.WhisperingVoice.com/TellMe

This book was set in Elegant Garamond by Emigré

Book and Cover Design by Steed Studios

Title Art by Dennis Millard